A Pigeon in Paris

PETITE TAKES FLIGHT

Written by PAIGE HOWARD

and Illustrated by JOANIE STONE

PUBLISHED by SLEEPING BEAR PRESS™

On the very first day of May,
a pigeon flew into Paris.
And even though the sky was gray
and the clouds were heavy with rain,
the pigeon knew, for now, Paris was home.

The next morning, bright and early, the pigeon began searching the parks and sidewalks of Paris for the sticks and scraps to build her nest.

The pigeon knew she had eggs to lay and babies on the way. When they arrived, they would need a nest to keep them warm and safe.

It wasn't too long before the eggs hatched
and the babies arrived.

The pigeon named them

CHÉRIE,

BISOU,

and *PETITE.*

They were chirpy and bright.
Hungry all day and hungry all night.

Chérie, Bisou, and Petite
were growing fast.

Their feathers were
getting thicker,

their legs were
growing longer,

and their wings were
spreading wider.

It was on a sunny morning that the pigeon
gathered her babies close and said,

"Little ones, today is the **day**!
Your feathers are thick enough,
your legs are long enough,
and your wings spread wide enough.
Today is the **day** you will learn to fly!"

First, Chérie stepped up to the brim of the nest,
spread her wings, and with a little bend in her legs,
she leaped up—

and out Chérie went!

Next, Bisou waddled up to the very brim of the nest,
spread his wings wide, bent his legs, and then jumped.

Up and away Bisou flew!

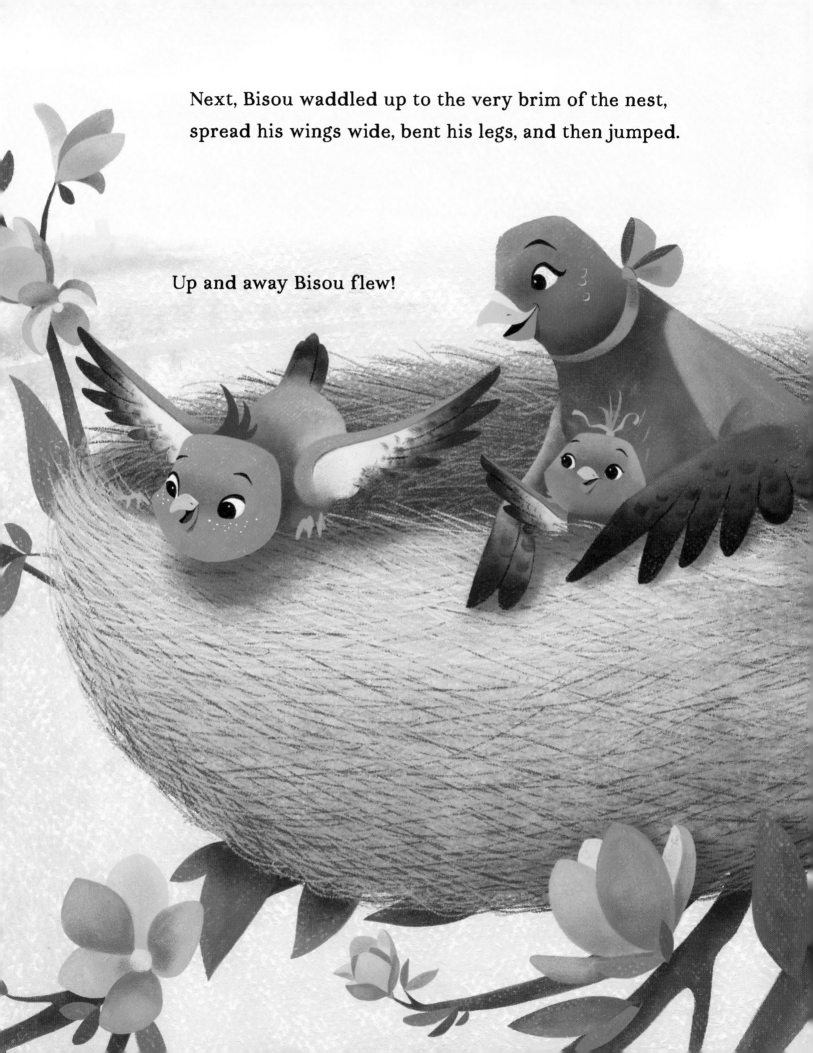

Now it was Petite's turn. With a little nudge from her mother,
Petite tiptoed up to the very, very brim of the nest,
put a little bend in her legs, puffed up her chest,
and spread her wings as wide as she possibly could.
Then, just as Petite went to jump up and out of the nest
like her siblings had . . .

she could not!

Petite's legs began to shake. Her wings pulled back. Her chest was no longer puffed up and the little pigeon felt deflated and small. Petite crept away from the edge of the nest and back in close to her mother.

"I cannot fly, Mama!" she cried.

"I cannot **and** I will not.
I am going to stay right here
in this nest with you."

"Okay, my little one," said Mama Pigeon.
"You **did** very well today.
Now it's time for a good meal and a long night's rest.
We will try again in the morning."

Later that night, as she cuddled up to her mother, her belly full and her eyes heavy, the little pigeon thought to herself,

**"I'm afraid to fly. I cannot fly.
I will not leave this little nest."**

When Petite woke up, to her surprise, she was alone in the nest.
Petite crooked her neck and stared up into the tall branches above her.
Her mother was nowhere to be seen.

Finally, she looked out beyond her tree and
saw her mother with her brother and sister across the way.

Bisou and Chérie were perched on a tree limb,
picking at a tasty worm, while Mama Pigeon
scoured the grass below for more food.

"Growwwwwlllll,"
went her belly!

Petite jumped, startled.
She was SO hungry!

"I'm hungry! I'm hungry!"
Petite called out to her family.

"Fly, Petite!" hollered Chérie.

"Fly! Fly!" yelled Bisou.

"You will have to fly or you will have to wait
until I get back to the nest.
It's up to you," Mama Pigeon called out.

Petite gently rubbed her belly. The little pigeon was
so hungry, but she was still too scared to fly . . .

so she would have to wait.

The next morning, a fog surrounded the nest.
Petite sighed and thought, "No flying for me today!"
But her mother had a different idea.

"Okay, Petite," said Mama Pigeon. "Today is the day!
Hop up to the very, very, VERY brim of the nest
and spread your wings."

"But Mama," Petite replied,
"it's foggy outside and I **cannot fly. I will not fly.**
Today is NOT the **day.** I will not leave this little nest."

"My sweet Petite," said Mama Pigeon
as she pulled Petite under her wing.
"There will be cloudy days.
There will be sunny days.
Most days will have a little bit of both.
No matter what, you will need to be able to fly."

Mama Pigeon released Petite from under her wing,
and with a gentle push toward the brim of the nest,
she whispered, "Today is the day, mon amour.

Today IS the day."

Again, Petite crept forward.
She closed her eyes tight,
spread her wings,
puffed up her chest,
and crouched low, bending her shaking legs
as best she could.

The next thing Petite knew,
she was up and out of the nest!

Her brother, sister, and mother
met her in the sky,

and Petite was not alone!

She was flying.

She was really flying!

Then, out of the corner of her eye, Petite saw her nest below,
and feeling like a little pigeon—much too little to fly!—
her wings stopped flapping.

Down,

down,

down Petite fell,

through the top of the tree,

through the branches,

through so many leaves,
toward the ground below.

"Fly!"
yelled her brother.

"Flap your wings!"
instructed Chérie.

And Petite heard them.
Spreading her wings wide,
she soared again,
lifting high into the sky.

Above her nest, above her brother and sister
and her very proud mother.

And, for the first time, Petite felt happy and free . . .

and not so little.

There would be many more
high-soaring flights for Petite,
and many more challenges she would face.
But whenever she started thinking:
CANNOT! WILL NOT! WON'T!
She would remind herself:
Even if you're afraid, in fact,
you absolutely CAN. And you WILL.
And although you may fall, you just get back up,
you spread your wings wide, and you

Fly, Fly, Fly!

For my Mama Pigeon,
Cheryl Alley Howard
—Paige

For Ruby,
who welcomed me into her nest
—Joanie

Text Copyright © 2023 Paige Howard
Illustration Copyright © 2023 Joanie Stone
Design Copyright © 2023 Sleeping Bear Press

SLEEPING BEAR PRESS™

2395 South Huron Parkway, Suite 200, Ann Arbor, MI 48104
www.sleepingbearpress.com © Sleeping Bear Press
Printed and bound in the United States
10 9 8 7 6 5 4 3 2 1
Library of Congress Cataloging-in-Publication Data
Names: Howard, Paige, 1985- author. | Stone, Joanie, illustrator.
Title: A pigeon in Paris : Petite takes flight / written by Paige Howard ;
illustrated by Joanie Stone.
Description: Ann Arbor, MI : Sleeping Bear Press, [2023] | Audience: Ages 4-8. |
Summary: Little pigeon Petite is too scared to join her siblings for their first
flight, but with her family's encouragement she finally tries--falls--and
learns a lesson about fear, failure, and strength that will carry her through life.
Identifiers: LCCN 2022037905 | ISBN 9781534111820 (hardcover)
Subjects: CYAC: Pigeons--Fiction. | Fear--Fiction. | Failure--Fiction. |
Self-confidence--Fiction. | Paris (France)--Fiction. | France--Fiction.
| LCGFT: Animal fiction. | Picture books.
Classification: LCC PZ7.1.H6879 Pi 2023 | DDC [E]--dc23
LC record available at https://lccn.loc.gov/2022037905